Disney
PRINCESS

3D

Cinderella and the Lost Mice

PaRRagon

Bath • New York • Singapore • Hong Kong • Cologne • Delhi
Melbourne • Amsterdam • Johannesburg • Auckland • Shenzhen

This edition published by Parragon in 2011

Parragon
Queen Street House
4 Queen Street
Bath BA1 1HE, UK

ISBN 978-1-4454-2591-7

Printed in China

Cinderella and the Lost Mice

PaRragon

Bath • New York • Singapore • Hong Kong • Cologne • Delhi
Melbourne • Amsterdam • Johannesburg • Auckland • Shenzhen

Welcome to your Princess 3D adventure.

Look at Gus the mischievous mouse. Put on your 3D glasses and it looks as if he is really scurrying around!

Turn the page to discover the magical story of *Cinderella and the Lost Mice*, and how her dreams come true.

Cinderella and the Lost Mice By E.C. Llopis
Illustrated by: IBOIX and Michael Inman

The stars twinkled in the clear night sky as the Prince twirled Cinderella outside to dance.

"Are you cold, my dear?" the Prince asked his princess.

"Just a bit, but –"

Smiling, the Prince reached for a box he had hidden under a bench. Inside was a beautiful winter coat.

"Oh, it's simply lovely!" Cinderella exclaimed. "Thank you!"

The next morning Cinderella showed her coat to Suzy the mouse. "Isn't the prince kind to me?" she said.

"Nice-a! Nice-a!" Suzy nodded and nuzzled the warm coat.

Cinderella didn't notice that Suzy had just come in from the cold. The tiny mouse shivered even though the room was warm!

Just then, Gus and Jaq scampered up onto Cinderella's dressing table. "Cinderelly! Cinderelly!" they chattered.

Cinderella didn't hear them as she rushed off to meet the Prince. She didn't know that they were cold, too!

Soon several more cold and shivering mice entered the room. They sat in front of the fire until their teeth stopped chattering. The poor mice had spent the night in the freezing attic! They hoped Cinderella would let them stay in her warm room. But there was a problem.

"Shoo, shoo!" The cruel housekeeper barged into the room and began chasing the mice! "You're making the whole castle dirty!" she shouted. "I should have the gardener haul you away!"

She was the reason that the mice were cold – and scared! They stayed in the attic to hide from her!

The mice scrambled back to the chilly attic,
not knowing where else to go.
"Cinderelly," Gus sighed. They needed
her help!

Suddenly – WHAM! – the gardener slammed cages over the mice and scooped them up!

"Now take them outside!" shrieked the housekeeper. "Take them far enough away that they never return!"

Of course, Cinderella had no idea what had happened as she and the Prince strolled along the castle grounds.

"Let's go to the stables!" Cinderella said suddenly. "We can say hello to the horses."

"And maybe take a ride?" the Prince asked hopefully.

"Lovely idea!" Cinderella replied.

Soon Cinderella and the Prince were riding through the countryside near the castle. They saw the gardener doing something in one of the fields.

"Hello!" shouted the Prince. "It's too cold to be working outside!"

But the gardener didn't seem to hear the Prince.

When the Prince and Princess returned to the stables, the Prince asked, "Do you think the gardener was acting oddly?"

"Perhaps he was distracted," Cinderella replied thoughtfully. "It must be hard to do much gardening when the ground is frozen."

But the gardener was not distracted about gardening. He was worried about the mice! He knew that they would freeze in the fields.

"All right." he said to his helpers. "Now don't mention this to the housekeeper, but I want to bring these poor mice to the stables."

So they took the grateful mice to their new home and even fed them.

The mice nestled together in the barn, but as night approached, they just got colder. Finally the horses allowed them to snuggle up in their manes to keep warm.

"Thassa nice-a," Gus said sleepily.

Meanwhile, Cinderella was beginning to worry. Where were her little friends?

"Jaq and Gus!" she thought suddenly. "They wanted to talk to me this morning, but I left in a rush to see the Prince. I wonder if they needed to tell me something."

"Don't worry, my dear. The mice have found a new friend." The Prince then told Cinderella about the gardener and what he had done.

Together, Cinderella and the Prince went to the stables to thank the gardener. Then Cinderella awakened the mice who were snuggled comfortably in the horses' manes.

A few nights later, there was a grand ball – with the gardener as the guest of honour. The cruel housekeeper now peeled potatoes in the kitchen. She would not be bothering the mice again. Meanwhile, the mice celebrated with a banquet of their own. And as for the horses, they got extra apples all around!

Look at all the things below that help Cinderella get to the ball.
Can you match each one with its shadow?

Cinderella leaves the ball in such a hurry that she loses a glass slipper!
Help Prince Charming through this maze to find Cinderella.
Look out for Anastasia and Drizella on the way!

START

FINISH

Answer:

Look at Cinderella in her beautiful ball gown.
Can you spot the 4 differences between the two pictures below?

Answer:

Which line leads Cinderella to the Fairy Godmother?

Poor Cinderella has so much work to do!
Help Gus and Jaq find their way through the maze to help Cinderella
finish her chores. Don't bump into Lucifer on the way!

START

FINISH

Answer:

Cinderella and her friends are making a dress for the ball.
How many pink cotton reels can you find hidden in this picture?

Gus and Jaq have organized a wonderful evening for Cinderella.
Can you match the right puzzle piece to the
missing parts of the picture?

A

B

C

1

2

3